THE MAGIC RING

A Picture Story From Yugoslavia

Retold by

MATIJA VALJAVEC

and

CENE VIPOTNIK

Illustrated by

MARLENKA STUPICA

THE WORLD PUBLISHING COMPANY

CLEVELAND AND NEW YORK

Published by The World Publishing Company
2231 West 110th Street, Cleveland, Ohio 44102
Published simultaneously in Canada by
Nelson, Foster & Scott Ltd.
First American Edition 1968
Library of Congress catalog card number: 68–14682
Copyright © 1957 by Mladinska Knjiga

ONCE UPON A TIME in a little house in the mountains there
lived a kind-hearted boy and his old widowed mother. They were
very, very poor. All they owned was the cottage they lived in and an
old gray cow. Every day the boy put the old gray cow out to graze in
the meadow. Then he gathered dry sticks for firewood and carried
them down to the village to sell. With the money he got for the
firewood he bought bread for himself and his mother.

One day he carried a bundle of firewood to the village as usual,
sold it, bought a loaf of bread, and started home with it. But on the
way he met some shepherd boys who were beating a little puppy. He
felt sorry for the poor creature, so he went up to the shepherd boys
and said:

"Look here, please don't hurt that good little dog! Why don't you
give him to me?"

"All right!" said the shepherd boys. "You give us your bread and
we'll give you the dog."

The bargain was made; the boy gave them the loaf of bread and
they gave him the puppy. He put it under his arm and carried it
home. When he got there, his old mother asked him as usual, "Have
you sold the sticks and brought home some bread?"

"No, I haven't," answered the boy. "But I have brought a good
little dog. I had to give all my bread for him."

"You shouldn't have done that," his mother scolded him. "There
is scarcely enough for the two of us to eat. How shall we feed the
dog as well?"

"Oh, we'll manage," said the boy. "I'll go out again and collect some more sticks and take them to the village for sale. Then I shall buy more bread and we shall have plenty to eat—you and I and the little dog too."

And so once more he collected sticks, carried them down to the village, sold them, used the money to buy bread, and started to carry it home to his mother. But again it so happened that he met those same shepherd boys. This time they were beating a little cat. He felt sorry for the poor cat, so he went up to the shepherd boys and said:

"Look here, please don't hurt that good little cat. Why don't you give her to me?"

"How much will you give us for her?"

"This little loaf, if that will do."

"Well, all right!" said the shepherd boys, and they gave him the cat in exchange for the bread.

When he came home, his old mother asked him as usual, "Have you sold the sticks and brought home some bread?"

"No, I haven't, but I have brought this nice pussycat. I had to give all my bread to buy her."

"And what was the good of that?" his mother scolded. "There is scarcely enough for us to eat, and how are we to feed a cat as well?"

"Oh, it'll be all right," said the kind-hearted boy. "I'll go to the woods again for sticks and sell them in the village. Then we shall have enough to eat—you and I and the dog and the pussycat too."

Again he collected dry sticks and sold them in the village. With the money he bought some bread and started home with it to his mother. But again it so happened that he met the shepherd boys. This time they were beating a small snake. Although he didn't really like snakes very much, the boy felt sorry for this one, and so he went up to the shepherd boys and said to them:

"Please don't hurt that poor little snake! Why don't you give it to me?"

"Give us that loaf of bread, and we'll give you the snake!"

The boy gave them the loaf, took the snake, and set out for home with it. But suddenly the snake began to speak and it said to him, in human speech:

"Thank you, kind youth, for saving my life. Now I beg you to carry me home to my mother. Tell her you saved her daughter's life. She will reward you generously. She will offer you silver; she will offer you gold; but don't accept these things. Ask instead for the small ring that lies in the chimney corner. That is a magic ring. If you just tap it with your finger, twelve obedient knights will appear before you and ask you for orders. And instantly they will carry out any order you may give them."

So the boy carried the snake to her mother's house.

"I have brought you your daughter whose life I have saved," he told her.

Mother Snake was happy and she said, "God reward you a hundredfold! What can I give you in return?"

And she showed him chests and jars filled to overflowing with silver and gold. But the boy remembered what the little snake had told him and he said:

"Mother Snake, if it's all the same to you, just give me that small ring that lies in the chimney corner."

When the boy came home, his old mother asked, "Where have you been all this time? I am terribly hungry. Have you brought some bread?"

"No," he replied. "But I've brought something that's much better than bread." And he took out the magic ring and tapped it with his finger. Instantly twelve obedient knights appeared before him, asking his orders.

"Bring us such food as the vicar and squire eat on the biggest holiday of the year!" he commanded.

And no sooner had he said than it was done. So much wonderful food was set before them that the table groaned under the weight. And so they ate as they had never done before in their lives, mother and son and dog and cat. From that day on, the boy no longer had to collect firewood and offer it for sale, for now they had enough of everything.

As time passed this wealth went to the young man's head and made him wish for things he had never thought of having before. One day he saw the Emperor's beautiful daughter and at once he fell in love with her. That very day he sent his mother to the Emperor to ask for the hand of his daughter in marriage. But the Emperor's reply was, "Go back to your son, old woman, and tell him that if he can cut down that forest in front of my castle and change it into fields on which wheat shall ripen by tomorrow morning, and have flour ground from the wheat, and have pancakes made from the flour for my breakfast, then I will gladly give him my daughter to be his wife. But if he fails, I shall have his head cut off!"

The old mother came home in tears and told her son what the Emperor had decreed.

"Don't cry, Mother dear, all will work out for the best," said her son, and he tapped the magic ring with his finger. In a twinkling the twelve obedient knights stood before him ready to do his bidding.

When the Emperor got up the next morning he could hardly believe his eyes, for he saw that the forest had been changed into fields on which ripe wheat was rippling like waves on a lake, and at his door the old mother was waiting for him with freshly cooked pancakes. But instead of keeping his promise, the Emperor said:

"Go home to your son and tell him that if he can reshape those hills you see before you, and turn them into vineyards all planted with vines, and if the grapes ripen so that I may drink the wine of them tomorrow morning, I will gladly give him my daughter to be his wife. But if he fails, he shall hang on the gallows, a meal for the crows!"

The old mother came home in tears and gave her son the Emperor's message. But the young man said, "Don't cry Mother dear, all will be well." Then again he tapped the magic ring with his finger and told the twelve obedient knights what they must do.

And when the Emperor rose in the morning, he went over to the vineyards, sampled the luscious grapes, and tasted the sweet new wine which the old woman brought and served to him. But for all that, the Emperor still would not give his daughter to the youth, but sent his mother away with this message:

"Go back to your son and tell him that if on that plain spread out before us, he can build a castle equal to my own, and surround it with beautiful gardens and choice fruit trees—some in blossom and some in fruit—and to these trees he can bring pretty birds that shall sing the sweetest songs, and if he can also make a road from here to that new castle, then I will gladly give him my daughter to be his wife. But if he cannot do these things—beware, for his days are numbered!"

The old mother came home in tears and told her son word for word what the Emperor had said. But her son replied, "Don't cry, Mother dear, all will turn out well." And again he tapped the magic ring with his finger and told the twelve obedient knights what they must do. And this time, when the Emperor rose in the morning and saw that the young man did everything he had demanded, he gave orders to prepare for the wedding. And so the youth and the Emperor's beautiful daughter were married.

But just as they were about to have the wedding feast a Maharajah from the East arrived on a visit. The Emperor offered him many fine gifts. However, the wicked Maharajah asked only for the young bridegroom's ring, for he had guessed that it had magic powers, although the young man had tried to guard his secret from every living soul. And finally, through a clever trick, the Maharajah managed to slip the ring from the young man's finger. Immediately he tapped it with his finger and the twelve obedient knights appeared, ready to serve their new master.

"Carry this castle, the princess, and me far away beyond the sea!" he commanded them, and even as he said it, so it was done.

Angrily, the Emperor called the young man and ordered him to bring back the castle and the princess. But without the ring the poor youth did not have the power to do this, so the Emperor cast him into a dungeon.

The unhappy young man sighed bitterly, but no one heard him. Not a living soul pitied him except his dog and cat. Since he had saved their lives, they made up their minds to find him and help him. But how were they to get into a dungeon that had neither door nor window? The cat climbed onto the roof, and finally found a crack that she could creep through, and thus she reached her master.

"My poor pussy," said the young man to the cat. "Who will take care of you now? That wicked Maharajah stole my ring and carried all my possessions far beyond the sea. Oh, pussy dear, if only you could get that ring back for me, all would be well again!"

The cat heard and understood these words, and she went back to the dog and told him, and these two faithful friends were deter-

mined to help their kind master. Setting out toward the East, they
soon came to the edge of the sea. And suddenly, just in front of
them—splash!—a fish fell onto the beach. It had leaped too far out
of the water trying to catch a fly, and now it lay on the dry sand. At
first the cat was tempted to eat it, for she was very hungry, but the
dog felt sorry for the fish and begged her not to hurt it. So they
dropped the fish back into the sea and it swam merrily away.

The cat could not swim but the dog could, so the cat hopped on
the little dog's back, and the dog swam off across the sea. In this
way they finally came to the Maharajah's castle. Now the dog stayed
outside and waited while the cat went inside. The Maharajah and
the princess thought she was a charming little pet, and the Maharajah even brought her into his bedroom to sleep on a velvet pillow
on his bed. But the moment the Maharajah was fast asleep, the cat
drew the magic ring off his finger so gently that he never felt it.
Then she slipped lightly out through the window and found the
little dog. The two at once set out for the seashore.

"Now, dear pussycat," said the dog, "You had better put the ring

in my mouth. I am used to carrying things, but you might let it fall into the water!"

But the cat wanted to have all the credit for recovering the ring, so she would not agree to this. Instead, she kept the ring in her own mouth, and hopped on the dog's back, and they started back across the sea. And then a terrible thing happened. The precious ring slipped out of the cat's mouth and sank to the bottom of the sea. The cat did not dare tell the dog what had happened until they had reached the land, for fear he would be so angry that he would put her off his back and let her drown. But when they were safely on the shore she confessed that she had lost the ring. However, just when the dog was about to scold her, the fish they had dropped back into the sea came swimming to the shore, ready to repay them for their kindness. It had found the ring on the bottom of the sea and now it tossed it up onto the beach. The dog and cat thanked the fish and took up the ring and carried it to the dungeon. There the cat took it and, quickly climbing onto the roof, she dropped the ring through the crack down to the prisoner. Tinkle, tinkle . . . the ring landed on the

dungeon floor and rolled right up to the young man. Glad and grateful, he thanked his faithful dog and cat. Then he tapped the ring with his finger and at once the twelve obedient knights appeared and asked his orders.

"Bring something for me to eat, and something for the dog and cat who are outside. Then see to it that I am set free at once, and that my castle is brought back immediately, and the princess and the Maharajah with it."

As soon as he said it, so it happened. At once he was freed from the dungeon, and the castle stood on its former site, together with the princess, Maharajah, and all. The young man went into the castle. As soon as the princess caught sight of him she was overjoyed and she ran to him and threw her arms around his neck.

Then, at last, they made their wedding feast. It was a feast such as never was seen before; they ate and drank until all had had their fill. I know, for I was there myself.

But as for the wicked Maharajah, they threw him into the middle of the sea.